# THE *LIFESAVING* ADVENTURE OF SAM DEAL,

## SHIPWRECK RESCUER

BY *CANDICE RANSOM*
ADAPTATION BY *AMANDA DOERING TOURVILLE*
ILLUSTRATED BY *ZACHARY TROVER*

Graphic Universe™ • Minneapolis • New York

# INTRODUCTION

THE ISLANDS OFF THE COAST OF NORTH CAROLINA ARE CALLED THE OUTER BANKS. THEY ARE ALSO CALLED THE GRAVEYARD OF THE ATLANTIC. IN THE DAYS BEFORE SHIPS USED POWERFUL ENGINES, STORMS OFTEN DROVE SHIPS ASHORE ON THE ISLANDS. MANY SAILORS AND PASSENGERS LOST THEIR LIVES IN THE ANGRY SEAS. IN 1874, THE U.S. LIFE-SAVING SERVICE BUILT STATIONS ALONG THE BEACHES OF THE OUTER BANKS. EACH STATION WAS RUN BY A KEEPER AND A CREW OF SIX SURFMEN. THESE MEN RESCUED SHIPWRECK VICTIMS.

AFRICAN AMERICANS USUALLY HELD THE LOWEST RANK IN THE CREW—SURFMAN NUMBER SIX. THEY TOOK CARE OF THE HORSES AND COOKED FOR THE CREW. IN 1879, THE WHITE KEEPER OF PEA ISLAND STATION WAS FIRED. THE SUPERVISOR DECIDED TO HIRE AN AFRICAN AMERICAN, RICHARD ETHERIDGE, TO REPLACE HIM. ETHERIDGE WAS A FORMER SLAVE AND A CIVIL WAR VETERAN. HE HAD BEEN SURFMAN NUMBER SIX AT ANOTHER STATION. NO WHITE SURFMEN WOULD WORK FOR THE NEW KEEPER. SO ETHERIDGE PUT TOGETHER AN AFRICAN AMERICAN CREW. PEA ISLAND BECAME THE FIRST ALL-BLACK LIFESAVING STATION.

THIS IS THE STORY OF WHAT HAPPENED AT PEA ISLAND ONE STORMY OCTOBER NIGHT. TEN-YEAR-OLD SAM DEAL WAS NOT A REAL PERSON. BUT HE COULD HAVE BEEN ONE OF THE BOYS WHO LONGED TO BE A SURFMAN ON THE OUTER BANKS.

BUOY.
THE RESCUED PERSON INTO THOSE CANVAS BREECHES, AND HE'LL FLOAT.
HE'S ONLY GOT FIVE MINUTES TO DO THE NEXT PART OF THE DRILL.
TIME'S UP!

PUT HIM BEHIND ME ON GINGER.

THROUGH THE NIGHT, TEAMS OF SURFMEN SWAM OUT TO THE WRECK. THEY BROUGHT BACK ALL THE SURVIVORS.

I DON'T KNOW HOW TO THANK YOU ENOUGH. YOU AND YOUR CREW ARE HEROES.

WE'RE JUST DOING OUR JOBS, CAPTAIN GARDINER.

SAM WAS PROUD OF THE SURFMEN AND OF GINGER TOO. HIS LITTLE HORSE HAD BRAVED THE ROUGH WAVES. HE KNEW SHE'D BE A GREAT HORSE SOMEDAY.

# AFTERWORD

IN 1915, THE U.S. LIFE-SAVING SERVICE BECAME THE U.S. COAST GUARD. THE STATIONS ON THE OUTER BANKS WERE STILL USED FOR SEARCH-AND-RESCUE OPERATIONS. EVENTUALLY, THE STATIONS WERE SHUT DOWN AS MODERN RESCUE METHODS WERE DEVELOPED. PEA ISLAND STATION CLOSED IN 1947. THE U.S. GOVERNMENT AWARDED MEDALS TO MANY WHITE LIFESAVING CREWS. BUT THE SURFMEN OF PEA ISLAND STATION NEVER RECEIVED ANY RECOGNITION FOR THEIR BRAVERY.

RICHARD ETHERIDGE AND HIS MEN WERE MOST LIKELY OVERLOOKED BECAUSE THEY WERE AFRICAN AMERICAN. IN 1995, EIGHTH GRADER KATIE BURKART WROTE A LETTER TO PRESIDENT BILL CLINTON. SHE BELIEVED THE MEN DESERVED A GOLD LIFESAVING MEDAL OF HONOR. PRESIDENT CLINTON AND ADMIRAL ROBERT KRAMEK OF THE U.S. COAST GUARD AGREED.

IN 1996, ADMIRAL KRAMEK POSTHUMOUSLY AWARDED GOLD MEDALS TO RICHARD ETHERIDGE AND THE CREW OF PEA ISLAND STATION FOR THEIR BRAVE RESCUE OF THE E. S. *NEWMAN* PASSENGERS AND CREW. IT WAS NEARLY ONE HUNDRED YEARS AFTER THAT STORMY NIGHT IN OCTOBER 1896.

# FURTHER READING AND WEBSITES

AFRICAN AMERICANS IN THE UNITED STATES COAST GUARD
HTTP://WWW.USCG.MIL/HISTORY/ARTICLES/H_AFRICANAMERICANS.ASP

AFRICAN AMERICANS IN THE U.S. COAST GUARD PHOTO GALLERY
HTTP://WWW.USCG.MIL/HISTORY/USCGHIST/AFRICAN_AMERICAN_PHOTO_
GALLERY.ASP

KARWOSKI, GAIL. *MIRACLE: THE TRUE STORY OF THE WRECK OF THE SEA
VENTURE.* MINNEAPOLIS: MILLBROOK PRESS, 2004.

MARKLE, SANDRA. *RESCUES!* MINNEAPOLIS: MILLBROOK PRESS, 2006.

"RESCUE MEN": THE STORY OF THE PEA ISLAND SURFMEN
HTTP://RESCUEMENFILM.COM/

SCHULZ, ANDREA. *NORTH CAROLINA.* MINNEAPOLIS: LERNER PUBLICATIONS
COMPANY, 2002.

U.S. COAST GUARD AWARDS
HTTP://WWW.USCG.MIL/HISTORY/AWARDS/11OCT1896.ASP

U.S. COAST GUARD STATION PEA ISLAND
HTTP://WWW.USCG.MIL/HISTORY/STATIONS/PEAISLAND.ASP

U.S. LIFE-SAVING SERVICE HERITAGE ASSOCIATION
HTTP://WWW.USLIFE-SAVINGSERVICE.ORG/

WEATHERFORD, CAROLE BOSTON. *SINK OR SWIM: AFRICAN-AMERICAN
LIFESAVERS OF THE OUTER BANKS.* WILMINGTON, NC: COASTAL CAROLINA
PRESS, 1999.

## ABOUT THE AUTHOR

CANDICE RANSOM HAS WRITTEN MANY AWARD-WINNING FICTION AND NONFICTION BOOKS FOR CHILDREN AND YOUNG ADULTS. SHE HOLDS A MASTER OF FINE ARTS IN WRITING FROM VERMONT COLLEGE. SHE LIVES IN FREDERICKSBURG, VIRGINIA.

## ABOUT THE ADAPTER

AMANDA DOERING TOURVILLE HAS WRITTEN MORE THAN 40 BOOKS FOR CHILDREN. TOURVILLE IS GREATLY HONORED TO WRITE FOR YOUNG PEOPLE AND HOPES THAT THEY WILL LEARN TO LOVE READING AND LEARNING AS MUCH AS SHE DOES. WHEN NOT WRITING, TOURVILLE ENJOYS TRAVELING, PHOTOGRAPHY, AND HIKING. SHE LIVES IN MINNESOTA WITH HER HUSBAND AND GUINEA PIG.

## ABOUT THE ILLUSTRATOR

ZACHARY TROVER HAS BEEN DRAWING SINCE HE WAS OLD ENOUGH TO HOLD A PENCIL AND HASN'T STOPPED YET. YOU CAN FIND HIM LIVING SOMEWHERE IN THE MIDWEST WITH HIS EXTREMELY PATIENT WIFE AND TWO EXTREMELY IMPATIENT DOGS.

Text copyright © 2011 by Candice F. Ransom
Illustrations © 2011 by Lerner Publishing Group, Inc.

Graphic Universe™ is a trademark of Lerner Publishing Group, Inc.

Graphic Universe™
A division of Lerner Publishing Group, Inc.
241 First Avenue North
Minneapolis, MN 55401 U.S.A.

Website address: www.lernerbooks.com

Library of Congress Cataloging-in-Publication Data

Ransom, Candice F., 1952–
    The lifesaving adventure of Sam Deal, shipwreck rescuer / by Candice Ransom ; illustrator, Zachary Trover.
       p.   cm. — (History's kid heroes)
    Includes bibliographical references.
    Summary: In 1896, ten-year-old Sam Deal and Ginger, the wild horse he has tamed, assist an all-Black lifesaving crew as they attempt to rescue survivors of a shipwreck off North Carolina's Outer Banks.
    ISBN 978–0–7613–6177–0 (lib. bdg. : alk. paper)
    1. Graphic novels. [1. Graphic novels. 2. Shipwrecks—Fiction. 3. Wild horses—Fiction. 4. Horses—Fiction. 5. African Americans—Fiction. 6. Outer Banks (N.C.)—History—19th century—Fiction.] I. Trover, Zachary, ill. II. Title.
PZ7.7.R34 2011
363.12'3810916348—dc22                                                    2009051719

Manufactured in the United States of America
1—CG—7/15/10